You're Just What I Need

by Ruth Krauss

Pictures by Julia Noonan

HarperCollinsPublishers

To Andrew,

my first bundle

—J.N.

Special thanks to Liza and Allie Rawson
and Kate and Emma Jackson.

Library of Congress Cataloging-in-Publication Data

Krauss, Ruth.

    You're just what I need / by Ruth Krauss ; pictures by Julia Noonan.

        p.   cm.

    Summary: As a child hides beneath a blanket, Mother playfully wonders if the hidden bundle could be anything she needs.

    ISBN 0-06-027514-6. — ISBN 0-06-443561-X (pbk.)

    [1. Mother and child—Fiction.]   I. Noonan, Julia, ill.   II. Title.

PZ7.K875Yo   1998   96-48581

[E]—dc20   CIP

                                                                    AC

❖

You're Just What I Need

One morning a mother saw a strange
bundle under the blankets in her bed.
"What is it?" she said to herself.
"What can it be?"

"Can it be a bundle of laundry?

I think I don't need any laundry."

"No," the bundle replied.

"I'm not a bundle of laundry."

"Can it be a bundle of carrots?
I think I don't need
any carrots."

"No, no," the bundle replied.

"I'm not a bundle of carrots."

"Let me think again," the mother said to herself.
She stopped to think again. "Maybe it's a monkey?
I think I'm sure I don't need a monkey."

"No, no, no," the bundle replied.

"I'm not a monkey."

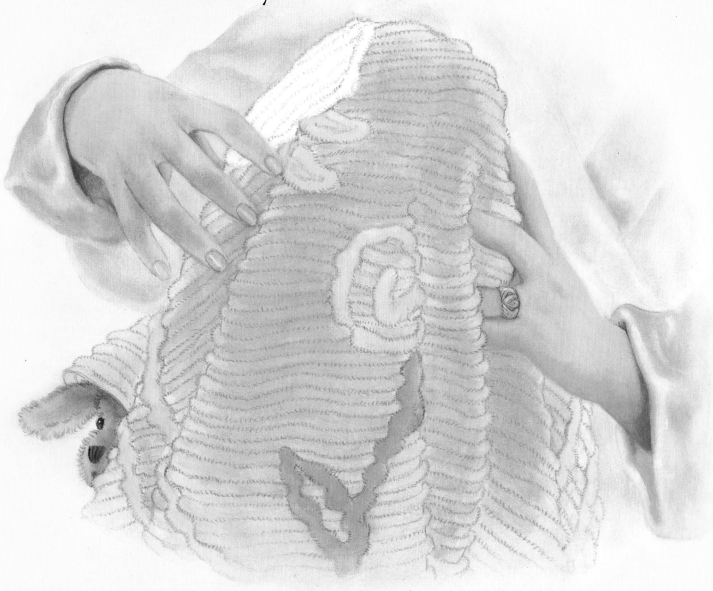

"Well, can you be Humpty-Dumpty?
I think I'm sure I don't need
Humpty-Dumpty either."

"No, no, no, no," the bundle replied. "I'm—

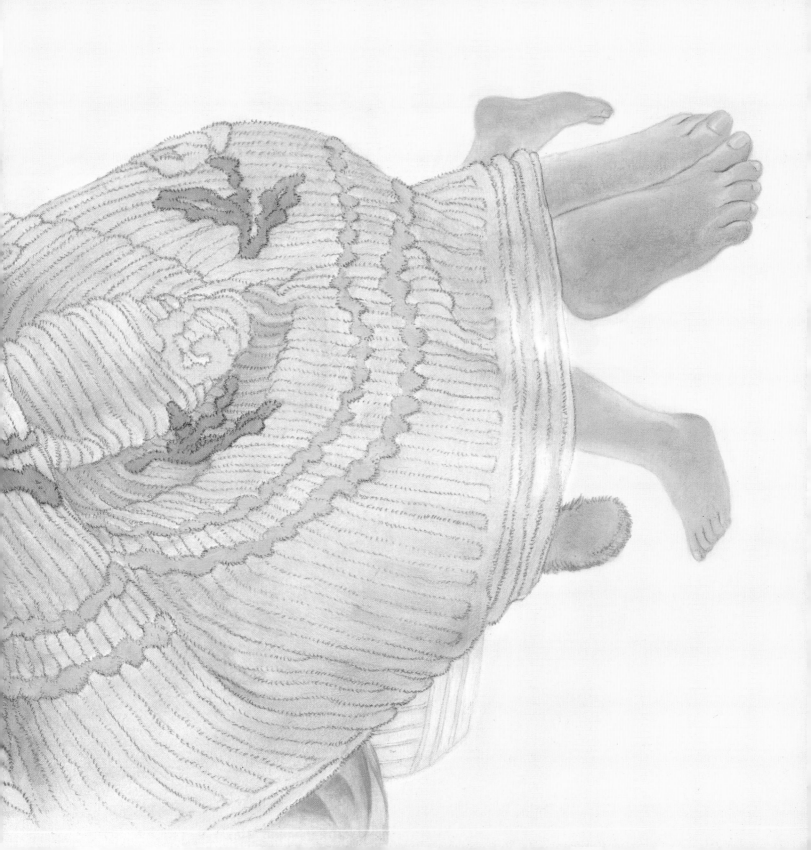

—not Humpty-Dumpty either."

"How about a bird?"

"No, no, no, no, no," the bundle replied.

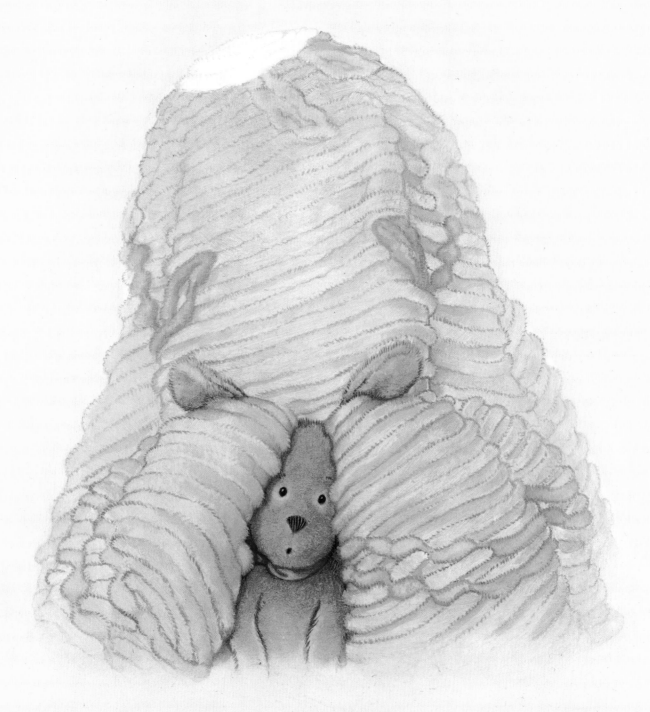

"Two birds?"

"No, no, no, no, no, no," the bundle replied.
Something began to show from under
the blankets, out one end of the bundle.

The mother pulled it.

"It looks like a mop. It feels like a mop," she said.

"No, no, no, no, no, no, NO," the bundle replied.

"Well, what is it? What can it be? What can you be? Tell me!" the mother said to the bundle.

Then up popped a head from the bundle
and yelled, "It's ME!"

"You!" the mother said. "Well, so it is!
So you are. It's you. And—
you're just what I need."